PETER RABBIT™ STORYTIME

TALES FROM BEATRIX POTTER

VOLUME TWO

F. WARNE & Co.

FREDERICK WARNE
Published by the Penguin Group
Penguin Books Ltd, 80 Strand, London WC2R 0RL, England
Penguin Young Readers Group, 375 Hudson Street, New York, New York 10014, USA
Penguin Books Australia Ltd, 250 Camberwell Road, Camberwell, Victoria 3124, Australia
Canada, India, New Zealand, South Africa

www.peterrabbit.com

First published by Frederick Warne 2005
3 5 7 9 10 8 6 4 2

Printed and bound in Malaysia

Contents

THE TALE OF
TWO BAD MICE

1904

ABOUT THIS BOOK

The Tale of Two Bad Mice was written at a particularly happy time for Beatrix Potter: she and her editor, Norman Warne, were becoming firm friends, and Beatrix was sometimes included in Warne family celebrations. Norman made a new cage for Beatrix's pet mice, Tom Thumb and Hunca Munca, so that she could more easily draw them for her new book. He had also made a doll's house for his favourite niece, Winifred, and Beatrix was invited to visit and sketch this too. However, her mother objected, and so Beatrix had to make do with photographs and examples of doll's furniture and food that Norman sent her. She kept some of the furniture all her life, and it can still be seen at Hill Top, her first Lakeland home.

Beatrix dedicated the book to Winifred: "For W.M.L.W., the little girl who had the doll's house."

ONCE upon a time there was a very beautiful doll's-house; it was red brick with white windows, and it had real muslin curtains and a front door and a chimney.

It belonged to two Dolls called Lucinda and Jane, at least it belonged to Lucinda, but she never ordered meals.

Jane was the Cook; but she never did any cooking, because the dinner had been bought ready-made, in a box full of shavings.

There were two red lobsters and a ham, a fish, a pudding, and some pears and oranges.

They would not come off the plates, but they were extremely beautiful.

One morning Lucinda and Jane had gone out for a drive in the doll's perambulator. There was no one in the nursery, and it was very quiet. Presently there was a little scuffling, scratching noise in a corner near the fire-place, where there was a hole under the skirting-board.

Tom Thumb put out his head for a moment, and then popped it in again.

Tom Thumb was a mouse.

A minute afterwards, Hunca Munca, his wife, put her head out, too; and when she saw that there was no one in the nursery, she ventured out on the oilcloth under the coalbox.

The doll's-house stood at the other side of the fire-place. Tom Thumb and Hunca Munca went cautiously across the hearthrug. They pushed the front door—it was not fast.

Tom Thumb and Hunca Munca went upstairs and peeped into the dining-room. Then they squeaked with joy!

Such a lovely dinner was laid out upon the table! There were tin spoons, and lead knives and forks, and two dolly-chairs—all *so* convenient!

Tom Thumb set to work at once to carve the ham. It was a beautiful shiny yellow, streaked with red.

The knife crumpled up and hurt him; he put his finger in his mouth.

"It is not boiled enough; it is hard. You have a try, Hunca Munca."

Hunca Munca stood up in her chair, and chopped at the ham with another lead knife.

"It's as hard as the hams at the cheesemonger's," said Hunca Munca.

The ham broke off the plate with a jerk, and rolled under the table.

"Let it alone," said Tom Thumb; "give me some fish, Hunca Munca!"

Hunca Munca tried every tin spoon in turn; the fish was glued to the dish.

Then Tom Thumb lost his temper. He put the ham in the middle of the floor, and hit it with the tongs and with the shovel—bang, bang, smash, smash!

The ham flew all into pieces, for underneath the shiny paint it was made of nothing but plaster!

Then there was no end to the rage and disappointment of Tom Thumb and Hunca Munca. They broke up the pudding, the lobsters, the pears and the oranges.

As the fish would not come off the plate, they put it into the red-hot crinkly paper fire in the kitchen; but it would not burn either.

Tom Thumb went up the kitchen chimney and looked out at the top—there was no soot.

While Tom Thumb was up the chimney, Hunca Munca had another disappointment. She found some tiny canisters upon the dresser, labelled—Rice—Coffee—Sago—but when she turned them upside down, there was nothing inside except red and blue beads.

Then those mice set to work to do all the mischief they could—especially Tom Thumb! He took Jane's clothes out of the chest of drawers in her bedroom, and he threw them out of the top floor window.

But Hunca Munca had a
frugal mind. After pulling
half the feathers out of
Lucinda's bolster, she
remembered that she herself
was in want of a feather bed.

With Tom Thumb's
assistance she carried the
bolster downstairs, and across
the hearthrug. It was difficult
to squeeze the bolster into
the mouse-hole; but they
managed it somehow.

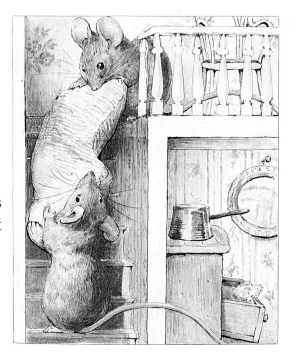

Then Hunca Munca went back and fetched a chair, a
book-case, a bird-cage, and several small odds and ends. The
book-case and the bird-cage refused to go into the mouse-hole.

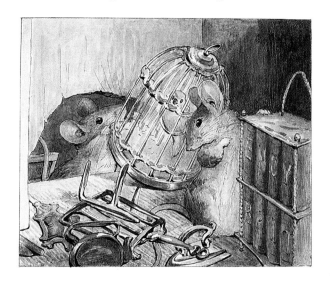

Hunca Munca left them behind the coal-box, and went to fetch a cradle.

Hunca Munca was just returning with another chair, when suddenly there was a noise of talking outside upon the landing. The mice rushed back to their hole, and the dolls came into the nursery.

What a sight met the eyes of Jane and Lucinda!

Lucinda sat upon the upset kitchen stove and stared; and Jane leant against the kitchen dresser and smiled—but neither of them made any remark.

The book-case and the bird-cage were rescued from under the coal-box—but Hunca Munca has got the cradle, and some of Lucinda's clothes.

THE TALE OF TWO BAD MICE

She also has some useful pots and pans, and several other things.

The little girl that the doll's-house belonged to, said,—"I will get a doll dressed like a policeman!"

But the nurse said,—"I will set a mouse-trap!"

So that is the story of the two Bad Mice,—but they were not so very very naughty after all, because Tom Thumb paid for everything he broke.

He found a crooked sixpence under the hearthrug; and upon Christmas Eve, he and Hunca Munca stuffed it into one of the stockings of Lucinda and Jane.

And very early every morning—before anybody is awake—Hunca Munca comes with her dust-pan and her broom to sweep the Dollies' house!

THE END

The Tale of
Mrs. Tiggy-Winkle

1905

ABOUT THIS BOOK

Although many of Beatrix Potter's story-book animals were based on her own pets, she often gave them human qualities too. The character of Mrs. Tiggy-winkle was inspired by Kitty McDonald, an old Scottish washerwoman, "a comical, round little old woman, as brown as a berry and wears a multitude of petticoats". She first told the story to her cousin Stephanie Hyde Parker in 1901, though it was eventually dedicated on publication in 1905 to Lucie Carr, daughter of the Vicar of Newlands, the valley in which the tale is set. Beatrix's tame hedgehog, Mrs. Tiggy-winkle, did her duty as a model: "So long as she can go to sleep on my knee she is delighted, but if she is propped up on end for half an hour, she first begins to yawn pathetically, and then she *does* bite! Nevertheless she is a dear person."

ONCE upon a time there was a little girl called Lucie, who lived at a farm called Little-town. She was a good little girl—only she was always losing her pocket-handkerchiefs!

One day little Lucie came into the farm-yard crying— oh, she did cry so! "I've lost my pocket-handkin! Three handkins and a pinny! Have *you* seen them, Tabby Kitten?"

The kitten went on washing her white paws; so Lucie asked a speckled hen— "Sally Henny-penny, have *you* found three pocket-handkins?"

But the speckled hen ran into a barn, clucking— "I go barefoot, barefoot, barefoot!"

And then Lucie asked Cock Robin sitting on a twig.

Cock Robin looked sideways at Lucie with his bright black eye, and he flew over a stile and away.

Lucie climbed upon the stile and looked up at the hill behind Little-town—a hill that goes up—up—into the clouds as though it had no top!

And a great way up the hill-side she thought she saw some white things spread upon the grass.

Lucie scrambled up the hill as fast as her stout legs would carry her; she ran along a steep path-way—up and up —until Little-town was right away down below—she could have dropped a pebble down the chimney!

Presently she came to a spring, bubbling out from the hill-side.

Someone had stood a tin can upon a stone to catch the water—but the water was already running over, for the can was no bigger than an egg-cup! And where the sand upon the path was wet—there were foot-marks of a *very* small person.

Lucie ran on, and on.

The path ended under a big rock. The grass was short and green, and there were clothes-props cut from bracken stems, with lines of plaited rushes, and a heap of tiny clothes pins—but no pocket-handkerchiefs!

But there was something else—a door! straight into the hill; and inside it some-one was singing—

"Lily-white and clean, oh!
With little frills between, oh!
Smooth and hot—red rusty spot
Never here be seen, oh!"

Lucie knocked—once—twice, and interrupted the song. A little frightened voice called out "Who's that?"

Lucie opened the door: and what do you think there was inside the hill?—a nice clean kitchen with a flagged floor and wooden beams—just like any other farm kitchen. Only the ceiling was so low that Lucie's head nearly touched it; and the pots and pans were small, and so was everything there.

There was a nice hot singey smell; and at the table, with an iron in her hand stood a very stout short person staring anxiously at Lucie.

Her print gown was tucked up, and she was wearing a large apron over her striped petticoat. Her little black nose went sniffle, sniffle, snuffle, and her eyes went twinkle, twinkle; and underneath her cap—where Lucie had yellow curls—that little person had PRICKLES!

"Who are you?" said Lucie. "Have you seen my pocket-handkins?"

The little person made a bob-curtsey—"Oh, yes, if you please'm; my name is Mrs. Tiggy-winkle; oh, yes if you please'm, I'm an excellent clear-starcher!" And she took something out of a clothes-basket, and spread it on the ironing-blanket.

"What's that thing?" said Lucie—"That's not my pocket-handkin?"

"Oh no, if you please'm; that's a little scarlet waist-coat belonging to Cock Robin!"

And she ironed it and folded it, and put it on one side.

Then she took something
else off a clothes-horse—

"That isn't my pinny?"
said Lucie.

"Oh no, if you please'm;
that's a damask table-cloth
belonging to Jenny Wren;
look how it's stained with
currant wine! It's very bad
to wash!" said Mrs. Tiggy-
winkle.

Mrs. Tiggy-winkle's
nose went sniffle, sniffle,
snuffle, and her eyes went
twinkle, twinkle; and she
fetched another hot iron
from the fire.

"There's one of my pocket-handkins!" cried Lucie—"And there's my pinny!"

Mrs. Tiggy-winkle ironed it, and goffered it, and shook out the frills.

"Oh that *is* lovely!" said Lucie.

"And what are those long yellow things with fingers like gloves?"

"Oh, that's a pair of stockings belonging to Sally Henny-penny—look how she's worn the heels out with scratching in the yard! She'll very soon go barefoot!" said Mrs. Tiggy-winkle.

"Why, there's another hand-kersniff—but it isn't mine; it's red?"

"Oh no, if you please'm; that one belongs to old Mrs. Rabbit; and it *did* so smell of onions! I've had to wash it separately, I can't get out the smell."

"There's another one of mine," said Lucie.

"What are those funny little white things?"

"That's a pair of mittens belonging to Tabby Kitten; I only have to iron them; she washes them herself."

"There's my last pocket-handkin!" said Lucie.

"And what are you dipping into the basin of starch?"

"They're little dicky shirt-fronts belonging to Tom Titmouse—most terrible particular!" said Mrs. Tiggy-winkle. "Now I've finished my ironing; I'm going to air some clothes."

"What are these dear soft fluffy things?" said Lucie.

"Oh those are woolly coats belonging to the little lambs at Skelghyl."

"Will their jackets take off?" asked Lucie.

"Oh yes, if you please'm; look at the sheep-mark on the shoulder. And here's one marked for Gatesgarth, and three that come from Little-town. They're *always* marked at washing!" said Mrs. Tiggy-winkle.

And she hung up all sorts and sizes of clothes—small brown coats of mice; and one velvety black mole-skin waist-coat; and a red tail-coat with no tail belonging to Squirrel Nutkin; and a very much shrunk blue jacket belonging to Peter Rabbit; and a petticoat, not marked, that had gone lost in the washing —and at last the basket was empty!

Then Mrs. Tiggy-winkle made tea—a cup for herself and a cup for Lucie. They sat before the fire on a bench and looked sideways at one another. Mrs. Tiggy-winkle's hand, holding the tea-cup, was very very brown, and very very wrinkly with the soap-suds; and all through her gown and her cap, there were *hair-pins* sticking wrong end out; so that Lucie didn't like to sit too near her.

When they had finished tea, they tied up the clothes in bundles; and Lucie's pocket-handkerchiefs were folded up inside her clean pinny, and fastened with a silver safety-pin.

And then they made up the fire with turf, and came out and locked the door, and hid the key under the door-sill.

Then away down the hill trotted Lucie and Mrs. Tiggy-winkle with the bundles of clothes!

All the way down the path little animals came out of the fern to meet them; the very first that they met were Peter Rabbit and Benjamin Bunny!

And she gave them their nice clean clothes; and all the little animals and birds were so very much obliged to dear Mrs. Tiggy-winkle.

So that at the bottom of the hill when they came to the stile, there was nothing left to carry except Lucie's one little bundle.

Lucie scrambled up the stile with the bundle in her hand; and then she turned to say "Good-night," and to thank the washer-woman—But what a *very* odd thing! Mrs. Tiggy-winkle had not waited either for thanks or for the washing bill!

She was running running running up the hill—and where was her white frilled cap? and her shawl? and her gown—and her petticoat?

And *how* small she had grown—and *how* brown—and covered with PRICKLES!

Why! Mrs. Tiggy-winkle was nothing but a HEDGEHOG.

*   *   *   *   *

(Now some people say that little Lucie had been asleep upon the stile—but then how could she have found three clean pocket-handkins and a pinny, pinned with a silver safety-pin?

And besides—*I* have seen that door into the back of the hill called Cat Bells—and besides *I* am very well acquainted with dear Mrs. Tiggy-winkle!)

THE END

THE TALE OF
MR. JEREMY FISHER

1906

ABOUT THIS BOOK

Mr. Jeremy Fisher had existed in Beatrix Potter's imagination for many years before his story was eventually published in 1906. He first appeared in 1893 in a picture letter to Eric Moore, written by Beatrix the day after she had sent the Peter Rabbit story to his brother Noel. In 1894, she produced a series of black-and-white frog drawings which were published in a children's annual and in 1902, Beatrix discussed Mr. Jeremy with her editor, Norman Warne. After Norman's death in 1905, Beatrix needed to work and took up the story with Harold, Norman's brother, as her new editor. "I feel as if my work and your kindness will be my greatest comfort." Perhaps the solitary hours spent sketching tranquil scenes in the Lake District did bring Beatrix comfort: the book certainly contains some of her most beautiful paintings. It is dedicated to Stephanie Hyde Parker, "from Cousin B."

ONCE upon a time there was a frog called Mr. Jeremy Fisher; he lived in a little damp house amongst the buttercups at the edge of a pond.

The water was all slippy-sloppy in the larder and in the back passage.

But Mr. Jeremy liked getting his feet wet; nobody ever scolded him, and he never caught a cold!

He was quite pleased when he looked out and saw large drops of rain, splashing in the pond—

"I will get some worms and go fishing
and catch a dish of minnows for my
dinner," said Mr. Jeremy Fisher.
"If I catch more than five fish,
I will invite my friends Mr.
Alderman Ptolemy Tortoise
and Sir Isaac Newton. The
Alderman, however, eats salad."

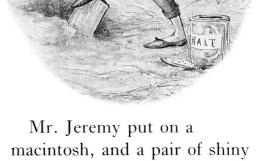

Mr. Jeremy put on a
macintosh, and a pair of shiny
goloshes;

he took his rod and basket, and
set off with enormous hops to
the place where he kept his boat.

The boat was round and green,
and very like the other lily-leaves.
It was tied to a water-plant in the
middle of the pond.

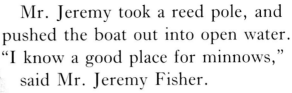

Mr. Jeremy took a reed pole, and pushed the boat out into open water. "I know a good place for minnows," said Mr. Jeremy Fisher.

Mr. Jeremy stuck his pole into the mud and fastened his boat to it.

Then he settled himself cross-legged and arranged his fishing tackle.

He had the dearest little red float. His rod was a tough stalk of grass, his line was a fine long white horse-hair,

and he tied a little wriggling worm at the end.

The rain trickled down his back, and for nearly an hour he stared at the float.

"This is getting tiresome, I think I should like some lunch," said Mr. Jeremy Fisher.

He punted back again amongst the water-plants, and took some lunch out of his basket.

"I will eat a butterfly sandwich, and wait till the shower is over," said Mr. Jeremy Fisher.

A great big water-beetle came up underneath the lily leaf and tweaked the toe of one of his goloshes.

Mr. Jeremy crossed his legs up shorter, out of reach, and went on eating his sandwich.

Once or twice something moved about with a rustle and a splash amongst the rushes at the side of the pond.

"I trust that is not a rat," said Mr. Jeremy Fisher; "I think I had better get away from here."

Mr. Jeremy shoved the boat out again a little way, and dropped in the bait. There was a bite almost directly; the float gave a tremendous bobbit!

"A minnow! A minnow! I have him by the nose!" cried Mr. Jeremy Fisher, jerking up his rod.

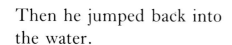

But what a horrible surprise! Instead of a smooth fat minnow, Mr. Jeremy landed little Jack Sharp the stickle-back, covered with spines!

The stickleback floundered about the boat, pricking and snapping until he was quite out of breath.

Then he jumped back into the water.

And a shoal of other little fishes put their heads out, and laughed at Mr. Jeremy Fisher.

And while Mr. Jeremy sat
disconsolately on the edge of his
boat—sucking his sore fingers and
peering down into the water—
a *much* worse thing happened;
a really *frightful* thing it would
have been, if Mr. Jeremy had
not been wearing a macintosh!

A great big enormous trout
came up—ker-pflop-p-p-p!
with a splash—

—and it seized Mr. Jeremy
with a snap, "Ow! Ow! Ow!"
—and then it turned and dived
down to the bottom of the pond!

But the trout was so displeased
with the taste of the macintosh,
that in less than half a minute it spat
him out again; and the only thing it
swallowed was Mr. Jeremy's goloshes.

Mr. Jeremy bounced up to the surface of the water, like a cork and the bubbles out of a soda water bottle; and he swam with all his might to the edge of the pond.

He scrambled out on the first bank he came to, and he hopped home across the meadow with his macintosh all in tatters.

"What a mercy that was not a pike!" said Mr. Jeremy Fisher.

"I have lost my rod and basket; but it does not much matter, for I am sure I should never have dared to go fishing again!"

He put some sticking plaster on his fingers, and his friends both came to dinner. He could not offer them fish, but he had something else in his larder.

Sir Isaac Newton wore his black and gold waistcoat.

And Mr. Alderman Ptolemy Tortoise brought a salad with him in a string bag.

And instead of a nice dish of minnows—they had a roasted grasshopper with lady-bird sauce; which frogs consider a beautiful treat; but *I* think it must have been nasty!

THE END

THE STORY OF
A FIERCE BAD RABBIT

1906

About This Book

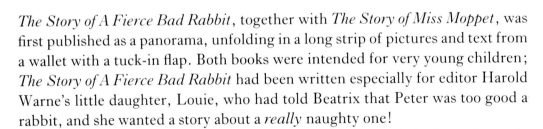

The Story of A Fierce Bad Rabbit, together with *The Story of Miss Moppet*, was first published as a panorama, unfolding in a long strip of pictures and text from a wallet with a tuck-in flap. Both books were intended for very young children; *The Story of A Fierce Bad Rabbit* had been written especially for editor Harold Warne's little daughter, Louie, who had told Beatrix that Peter was too good a rabbit, and she wanted a story about a *really* naughty one!

Unfortunately the panoramic format was not popular with the bookshops. As Beatrix wrote later: "The shops sensibly refused to stock them because they got unrolled and so bad to roll up again." In 1916, both stories were reprinted in book form and listed at the end of the series of Peter Rabbit books, alongside the nursery rhyme collections which were also intended for the very young.

THIS is a fierce bad Rabbit; look at his savage whiskers, and his claws and his turned-up tail.

This is a nice gentle Rabbit. His mother has given him a carrot.

The bad Rabbit would like some carrot.

He doesn't say "Please."
He takes it!

THE STORY OF A FIERCE BAD RABBIT

And he scratches the
good Rabbit very badly.

The good Rabbit
creeps away, and hides
in a hole. It feels sad.

This is a man with a gun.

He sees something sitting on a bench. He thinks it is a very funny bird!

He comes creeping up behind the trees.

And then he shoots—
BANG!

This is what happens—

But this is all he finds on the bench, when he rushes up with his gun.

The good Rabbit peeps out of its hole.

And it sees the bad Rabbit tearing past— without any tail or whiskers!

THE END

THE TALE OF
TIMMY TIPTOES

1911

ABOUT THIS BOOK

As Beatrix Potter's books continued to sell, she became known in America as well as Britain, receiving letters from eager readers far and wide. *The Tale of Timmy Tiptoes* was written to appeal to an American audience, with grey squirrels (which originally came to Britain from America), chipmunks and a black bear. Even the book's dedication shows the author departing from her usual very personal message to look further afield: "For many unknown little friends, including Monica." Monica was "the school friend of a little cousin, who asked for it as a favour, and the name took my fancy," as Beatrix explained later. By this time (1911), she was very occupied with farming and looking after her elderly parents, and Timmy Tiptoes' story was the only book to appear in that year.

ONCE upon a time there was a little fat comfortable grey squirrel, called Timmy Tiptoes. He had a nest thatched with leaves in the top of a tall tree; and he had a little squirrel wife called Goody.

Timmy Tiptoes sat out, enjoying the breeze; he whisked his tail and chuckled—"Little wife Goody, the nuts are ripe; we must lay up a store for winter and spring."

Goody Tiptoes was busy pushing moss under the thatch —"The nest is so snug, we shall be sound asleep all winter."

"Then we shall wake up all the thinner, when there is nothing to eat in spring-time," replied prudent Timothy.

When Timmy and Goody Tiptoes came to the nut thicket, they found other squirrels were there already.

Timmy took off his jacket and hung it on a twig; they worked away quietly by themselves.

Every day they made several journeys and picked quantities of nuts. They carried them away in bags, and stored them in several hollow stumps near the tree where they had built their nest.

When these stumps were full, they began to empty the bags into a hole high up a tree, that had belonged to a wood-pecker; the nuts rattled down—down —down inside.

"How shall you ever get them out again? It is like a money-box!" said Goody.

"I shall be much thinner before spring-time, my love," said Timmy Tiptoes, peeping into the hole.

They did collect quantities —because they did not lose them!

Squirrels who bury their nuts in the ground lose more than half, because they cannot remember the place.

The most forgetful squirrel in the wood was called Silver-tail. He began to dig, and he could not remember. And then he dug again and found some nuts that did not belong to him; and there was a fight. And the other squirrels began to dig—the whole wood was in commotion!

Unfortunately, just at this time a flock of little birds flew by, from bush to bush, searching for green caterpillars and spiders. There were several sorts of little birds, twittering different songs.

The first one sang—"Who's bin digging-up *my* nuts? Who's-been-digging-up *my* nuts?"

And another sang—"Little bit-a-bread and-*no*-cheese! Little bit-a-bread an'-*no*-cheese!"

The squirrels followed and listened. The first little bird flew into the bush where Timmy and Goody Tiptoes were quietly tying up their bags, and it sang—"Who's-bin digging-up *my* nuts? Who's been digging-up *my*-nuts?"

Timmy Tiptoes went on with his work without replying; indeed, the little bird did not expect an answer. It was only singing its natural song, and it meant nothing at all.

But when the other squirrels heard that song, they rushed upon Timmy Tiptoes and cuffed and scratched him, and upset his bag of nuts. The innocent little bird which had caused all the mischief, flew away in a fright!

Timmy rolled over and over, and then turned tail and fled towards his nest, followed by a crowd of squirrels shouting—"Who's-been digging-up *my*-nuts?"

They caught him and dragged him up the very same tree, where there was the little round hole, and they pushed him in. The hole was much too small for Timmy Tiptoes' figure. They squeezed him dreadfully, it was a wonder they did not break his ribs. "We will leave him here till he confesses," said Silvertail Squirrel, and he shouted into the hole— "Who's-been-digging-up *my*-nuts?"

Timmy Tiptoes made no reply; he had tumbled down inside the tree, upon half a peck of nuts belonging to himself. He lay quite stunned and still.

Goody Tiptoes picked up the nut bags and went home. She made a cup of tea for Timmy; but he didn't come and didn't come.

Goody Tiptoes passed a lonely and unhappy night. Next morning she ventured back to the nut-bushes to look for him; but the other unkind squirrels drove her away.

She wandered all over the wood, calling—

"Timmy Tiptoes! Timmy Tiptoes! Oh, where is Timmy Tiptoes?"

In the meantime Timmy Tiptoes came to his senses. He found himself tucked up in a little moss bed, very much in the dark, feeling sore; it seemed to be under ground. Timmy coughed and groaned, because his ribs hurted him. There was a chirpy noise, and a small striped Chipmunk appeared with a night light, and hoped he felt better?

It was most kind to Timmy Tiptoes; it lent him its night-cap; and the house was full of provisions.

The Chipmunk explained that it had rained nuts through the top of the tree—"Besides, I found a few buried!" It laughed and chuckled when it heard Timmy's story. While Timmy was confined to bed, it 'ticed him to eat quantities— "But how shall I ever get out through that hole unless I thin myself? My wife will be anxious!" "Just another nut— or two nuts; let me crack them for you," said the Chipmunk. Timmy Tiptoes grew fatter and fatter!

Now Goody Tiptoes had set to work again by herself. She did not put any more nuts into the wood-pecker's hole, because she had always doubted how they could be got out again. She hid them under a tree root; they rattled down, down, down. Once when Goody emptied an extra big bagful, there was a decided squeak; and next time Goody brought another bagful, a little striped Chipmunk scrambled out in a hurry.

"It is getting perfectly full-up downstairs; the sitting-room is full, and they are rolling along the passage; and my husband, Chippy Hackee, has run away and left me. What is the explanation of these showers of nuts?"

"I am sure I beg your pardon; I did not know that anybody lived here," said Mrs. Goody Tiptoes; "but where is Chippy Hackee? My husband, Timmy Tiptoes, has run away too."

"I know where Chippy is; a little bird told me," said Mrs. Chippy Hackee.

She led the way to the wood-pecker's tree, and they listened at the hole.

Down below there was a noise of nut crackers, and a fat squirrel voice and a thin squirrel voice were singing together—

"My little old man and I fell out,
How shall we bring this matter
    about?
Bring it about as well as you can,
And get you gone, you little old
    man!"

"You could squeeze in, through that little round hole," said Goody Tiptoes.

"Yes, I could," said the Chipmunk, "but my husband, Chippy Hackee, bites!"

Down below there was a noise of cracking nuts and nibbling; and then the fat squirrel voice and the thin squirrel voice sang—

"For the diddlum day
Day diddle dum di!
Day diddle diddle dum day!"

Then Goody peeped in at the hole, and called down—"Timmy Tiptoes! Oh fie, Timmy Tiptoes!" And Timmy replied, "Is that you, Goody Tiptoes? Why, certainly!"

He came up and kissed Goody through the hole; but he was so fat that he could not get out.

Chippy Hackee was not too fat, but he did not want to come; he stayed down below and chuckled.

And so it went on for a fortnight; till a big wind blew off the top of the tree, and opened up the hole and let in the rain.

Then Timmy Tiptoes came out, and went home with an umbrella.

But Chippy Hackee continued to camp out for another week, although it was uncomfortable.

At last a large bear came walking through the wood. Perhaps he also was looking for nuts; he seemed to be sniffing around.

Chippy Hackee went home in a hurry!

And when Chippy Hackee got home, he found he had caught a cold in his head; and he was more uncomfortable still.

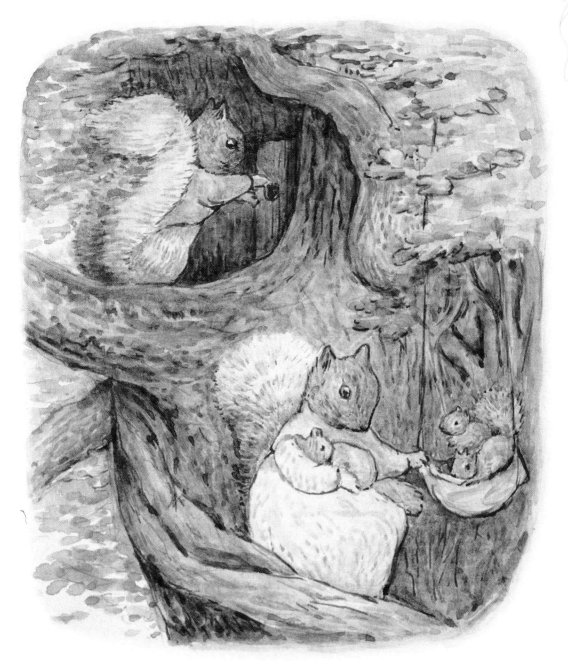

And now Timmy and Goody Tiptoes keep their nut-store fastened up with a little padlock.

And whenever that little bird sees the Chipmunks, he sings—"Who's-been-digging-up *my*-nuts? Who's been digging-up *my*-nuts?"

But nobody ever answers!

THE END